On His Knees

A GENTLE FEMDOM EROTIC ROMANCE

IRIS TROVAO

WWW.EMILYSHURRICANE.COM

Copyright © 2022 by Iris Trovao

All rights reserved.

No part of this book may be reproduced in any form or by any electronic or mechanical means, including information storage and retrieval systems, without written permission from the author, except for the use of brief quotations in a book review.

Cover Design: Emily S Hurricane

Editor: Emerald Baynton

Blurb Doctor: Alexandria Lee

ISBN: 9798359412384

Chapter One

ANNIKA SAT IN FRONT OF THE LUSH RED CURTAIN, wondering how the fuck she'd gotten to the point that she'd willingly put herself in a box. She tapped her foot impatiently, the sound near-deafening in the small room. When it grew to be annoying, she crossed her legs to get her heel off of the floor.

Within seconds, her suede shoe began to wiggle, anxiety making it tap in the air instead.

She huffed. *It's not like this is going to do anything. I'm not going to find what I'm looking for here.*

But...she couldn't tell her friends that. How could she? How could she tell them that she hadn't been with someone in so long because she was looking for a man that didn't exist? That she had needs that she'd never actually be able to fulfil, and she was getting to the point where she was ready to give up?

She was so tired of dating and having to pretend. Or, *not* pretending, and scaring them off. So it was either live a lie or live alone.

And though at this point it seemed preferable to just live

alone, she did very much love her friends. Gianna and Taylor meant well, and just wanted to see her happy. They'd put a lot of time and effort into getting her here, so she had to at least honour that. What were a few blind dates to appease those most important to her?

There was a light knock at the door behind Annika, and she startled. The noise was supposed to be coming from behind the curtain, not from the hallway.

"Sorry to bother you, miss." The voice through the door was soft and muffled, but formal. "It's security. May I have a word?"

She could have reached the lock from her plush seat, but she opted to stand to face the man outside. She silently prayed that security was knocking on her door because they had to evacuate or something, and she could just get out of this.

She opened the door, and her heart rate tripled. He was a security guard, all right. Body-hugging black jeans, a t-shirt that cupped his sculpted muscles like it had been painted on. He had a strong jaw, dressed with sandy stubble, but a set of surprisingly soft-looking lips for his beastly frame.

When those lips curled into a genuine smile, his light green eyes smiled with them, capturing her like a hunter's snare.

Then he glanced down at his clipboard, the moment over, and Annika blinked rapidly, amazed at how quickly she'd been distracted by his sweetness.

He ran a pencil down his list. "You're...Annika?"

Her name rolling off of his tongue did things to her libido, and she wished so badly that guys like this were into what she was into. Seeing him on his knees before her, those big eyes looking up as she stroked his hair and told him—

Focus, focus, she thought frantically. "Yes, that's me," she replied, hoping she sounded like she *didn't* have lurid images flitting through her mind.

"Good." There was that smile again. "I'm Ben, security for this hall. I prefer to introduce myself before the ladies enter the rooms, but you arrived early and I missed you." His formal way of speaking came off professional but natural, as if he'd been doing this job a long time.

"Sorry," she replied with a little wince. "My friends kind of talked me into this, and to be honest I figured I'd rather wait in here than listen to how *excited* they are for me while we waited to be collected. So I found my room number on the list."

He shook his head. "No apologies necessary. I just like to make sure that everyone knows who I am, in case you need anything. This is your first time, correct?"

She nodded. "Yes." She bit back the part about how Taylor had done this a bunch of times before, giving her a detailed rundown of how it all worked. Annika was enjoying looking at this guy, and if he was going to explain how the event worked, she was down for watching him do it.

"Alright, so, behind that curtain is a glass panel." He motioned past her with the pencil, and she glanced over her shoulder at where he was pointing. "There's another curtain on the other side. There's an intercom system so you can speak with the person on the other side, but you can only see each other if you both consent and open your curtains." He tucked the pencil behind his ear and relaxed the arm with the clipboard as she turned back to him. "There's a red button on the left side of your chair, and if you need any help, you reach down and press it then a light will go on above your door and I'll come in."

Annika couldn't help the small smirk that played her lips. "*Any* help?"

His cheeks pinked, and she couldn't believe the cuteness of such a burly man blushing. "Yes, whatever you need," he said, and the words reverberated inside of her, an echo of her earlier fantasies.

She cleared her throat nervously. "Well, thank you," she said hoarsely, "Ben."

"You're welcome," he replied, and she didn't miss the slight edge to his voice, mirroring her own. He bowed his head a little before retreating to a small desk along the back of the hallway, taking his post next to it.

Annika watched him set down the clipboard and clasp his hands together, cords of muscle in his forearms rippling as he took a guard pose. She clicked her door shut before she could gawk any harder, resisting the urge to fan herself.

Seriously, has it been that long that I'm simping over the first hot dude I see? Not to mention, he's not one of the eligible bachelors I'll be meeting with, so he's kinda off-limits. How cringey is it to hit on staff at a bar?

She sighed and flopped down in her chair. It didn't matter, anyway. As much as she lamented that guys never wanted to play the kinds of games she wanted to play, buff manly guys like *that* definitely didn't want to.

"Whatever you need," his husky voice echoed in her head, and her body temperature rose. How she longed to take him up on that. In ways that always made men run away from her.

She reached down and danced a finger over the security button, just to make sure that she knew where it was. Realistically, she imagined it wouldn't be something many would use. Aside from breaking the glass separating the rooms, what could someone on the other side really do that couldn't be fixed by the woman heading out into the hallway?

It was nice, though, to know that there was someone looking out for her. One never knew what kind of people lurked and preyed. And as much as she liked to think of herself as a badass, Annika wasn't so naive to think that her five-foot-four pleasantly plump frame was going to do much against most predators.

It wasn't the time to think about that, though. There was

a sexy-as-hell security guard in the hallway that was there specifically to protect damsels in distress. She just had to focus on getting through this process so she could have a couple of drinks with her friends and then go the hell home to cuddle up with the most important man in her life—her cat, Westley.

"Hello?" a voice came through the intercom, startling her. "I don't know how this thing works."

"I can hear you," Annika replied, lacing her fingers together over her knee. "Can you hear me?"

"Yeah," he replied. "This is so weird. I thought it would be like talking on speakerphone, but it's not at all."

She tilted her head back and forth. "It's kind of more like a drive-thru, where I don't know how loud I'm supposed to talk."

He laughed, dissolving a bit of the tension. "Well, your voice sounds perfect. It's so sexy."

She rolled her eyes. *That was fast.* "What's your name?"

"Luke, what's your name, beautiful?"

Ugh, real fast. "You don't even know what I look like," she scoffed. "At least when guys on social media slide into my DMs with a 'hi, beautiful' they've at least seen a profile picture."

He seemed to choke on his words, unsure of how to respond.

"So, let's try this again. Hi Luke, I'm Annika," she prompted, crossing her arms. "What do you do for a living?"

"This would be way nicer if I could see you," he replied. "Let's open the curtains."

She sighed. "Hard pass. I think you'd be better off in a different booth."

"Are you sure?" His voice was almost a whine.

"Do you have a little button on the left side of your chair?" she asked, gently circling her finger around the outside of hers.

He didn't answer for a moment, and then finally said, "...no?"

"Well I do," she replied. "And if I push it, a security guard with arms as big around as my head will forcibly remove you from the premises."

Luke didn't reply, simply grumbling to himself under his breath, and then fell silent. Annika assumed he'd left his booth. *The speakers could really use an OFF switch,* she thought. Being able to mute and unmute would be handy.

A metallic sound came through the speaker, and then knocking on the window startled her.

"Hey baby," a new voice slurred, louder as if it were closer to the speaker. "Open your curtain, I have something for you."

"Oh my *god.*" Annika got to her feet and left the room. Once in the hallway, she pressed her back against the door, staring up at the ceiling.

"Are you alright?" Ben asked, striding towards her from his post, his brow furrowed in concern.

She nodded jerkily, and then leaned her head back on the door, rolling it so she could look up at him. "You know I thought that this wouldn't be as bad as online dating?"

He chuckled. "Do I need to take care of the guy on the other side?" He inclined his head towards the booth.

"I'm fine, but he may or may not have his dick out, on the other side of that curtain." She flicked her wrist in the general direction of the offender. "So maybe someone should look into that if it's not something you guys want in here."

His expression like stone, he pressed a finger to his ear. "Room seven, potential exposure."

It took her a moment to realize that he had a hidden earbud, and she was glad she hadn't asked a dumb, *what?*

He listened for another moment and then lowered his hand, giving her a firm nod. "Taken care of, ma'am."

The respectful term made her belly flutter with butterflies, and she raised her chin a smidgen. "Thank you."

"Can I get you anything?"

A big tall glass of Ben? She smiled through her dirty thoughts. "If you have a glass of water kicking around, I wouldn't argue."

"I've got bottled, if that's okay?" He strode to the far side of his desk, and leaned over, opening a little mini-fridge beside it. "I also have some bottled juices and soft drinks. They don't allow alcohol or open glasses in the booths."

Annika took in the globes of his tight ass as he rummaged through the fridge, her mouth going dry. "Something fruity would be great," she called, mourning the loss of his perfect behind as he stood with a bottle in hand.

She read the label as he handed it over. It was strawberry-kiwi sparkling water, one of her favourite flavour combos, and she smiled brightly as she unscrewed the cap.

"Thank you, Ben."

"Very welcome, ma'am," he replied, before returning to his post.

She'd contemplated just outright leaving when she'd busted out of the booth...but was it worth another round of potential assholes to get to hang out with this guy some more? She knew it likely wouldn't lead to anything at all, but the thought of spending a bit of time hearing his *ma'am's* was like a soothing balm on her raging libido.

She took a sip of the delightfully sweet beverage he'd brought her, taking in his stoic frame one more time before slipping back into her booth.

Chapter Two

"Yeah, I'm definitely into submissive women, like, you know, she's gotta be cool with me being *the man,* you know?"

Pass.

"So what do you do for a living? I hope you're not a cop or something, I hate manly women."

Pass.

"I am not looking for a sexual relationship until after marriage."

Pass.

"I hate cats."

Pass!

Annika left the booth, glancing up and down the hall, brow furrowed.

"You alright?" Ben asked, and though he didn't move from his post, she could tell from his shoulders stiffening that he was concerned about her.

"Yeah, I'm fine, just can't remember which direction the bathroom is in?" She pointed both ways with finger guns. "Help a lady out?"

He inclined his head. "Just down this way," he said. "The only door on your left."

"Thanks." She flashed him a smile and hurried to the bathroom as fast as her heels would carry her. After relieving herself and washing her hands, she leaned over to check her makeup closer in the mirror. She'd rubbed her face enough times with exasperation in the booth that she wanted to make sure she wasn't all smudged up.

It seemed backwards to put on a face when she wasn't even letting these guys see her...but there was Ben. Even if nothing was going to happen between them, she was enjoying the flirting and couldn't help but want to look good. She leaned forward, adjusting her push-up bra a little, making sure her tits were pillowed just right in the V of her top.

Maybe it was silly, but she decided she might as well have a little fun.

She walked back to the booth slowly, pausing at his post and leaning against the wall opposite him. "Can you believe there are people out there that don't like cats?"

He cocked a brow. "I don't think I could trust a person that doesn't like cats."

Good answer, Annika thought, and crossed her ankles casually. "I'm losing faith in this process."

"Nobody catching your eye?"

Is it just my imagination, or does he sound hopeful? Her stomach tightened a little. It would be mean to lead him on. Although, even if he wasn't into the same things as her, a one night stand could be fun, right? She raked her eyes down the slope of his jaw.

"Well, they're not catching my ears, that's for sure," she joked, wrinkling her nose at her own lameness. *Yes, your severe wit will surely seduce this gorgeous man.*

He chuckled, whether out of pity or out of actual amusement, she wasn't sure. But he didn't seem put off by her.

"How long do you have to endure this before you feel like you've honoured your friends?" Ben asked, and she blinked at him in shock before she remembered she'd told him why she'd been in the booth so early.

"I'm that transparent, huh?" She ran a hand through her long dark curls, swiping a few errant locks behind her ear.

He shook his head. "I wouldn't say transparent, no," he said thoughtfully. "But you seem like the type to care enough about her friends' feelings to stick something out."

"I'm going to take that as a compliment." She pursed her lips and pointed at him, giving her best stern stare, though it lasted all of five seconds before she broke into a smile at the low rumble of his laugh.

"It was absolutely meant as one." He held up his hands, palms out. He pulled out his phone from his pocket, glancing at it and then flashing her the time. "You've got a half hour before the booths stop cycling, anyway. So if you haven't found your true love by then, no new potentials will enter."

"Oh, that is good news!" she replied with a grin. "Though I'll say, my true love is that strawberry kiwi drink you gave me. It's so delicious, thank you." Before she could stop herself, she reached a hand out and gave his bicep a squeeze. It was meant to be a casual gesture, just a little movement to accentuate the *thank you*, but at the feel of his hard-as-a-rock muscles beneath her fingers, heat flushed through her.

Oh, how she wanted this man beneath her. Baring his body, his throat, placing his utmost trust in her to bring him pleasure, teach him how to worship—

She dropped her hand, giving him an awkward smile and hoping that the moment hadn't stretched on so long that it was weird, and scurried back into her booth.

"Hey, do I hear some movement over there?" someone asked. "I was worried I'd scared you away before I arrived."

"Just had a little break," Annika said, taking her seat and

trying to push away all of the lurid Ben fantasies floating in her head.

"Well, I'm glad I caught you," came the reply. "You have a nice voice."

"Thank you." She paused, trying to decide what question she wanted to ask. She finally settled on, "What's your name?" She realized she was absently circling the security button, and jerked her hand away like it was on fire.

"I'm Jon, and you?"

"Annika."

"That's beautiful. And what do you do for a living, Annika?"

"I'm a vet tech," she said, and the words almost held no meaning because she'd said them so many times that night. "Like a nurse, but for a vet instead of a doctor."

"Oh, that's interesting." He sounded genuine, so that was at least a point if he was actually interested in her job and not just going through the motions. "So you love animals? I don't know if I could do that job. Isn't it hard if they die?"

She cocked a brow. An actual thoughtful question that had nothing to do with his dick. "It is...but it happens, and it's worth the risk to try to save them to be able to give someone back their pet."

"I guess someone has to do it, huh?"

"What do you do, Jon?" She crossed her legs, lacing her fingers over her thigh.

"You know, I've gotten laughed at a lot tonight about my job," he said, reluctance clear in his tone.

Annika cocked a brow. "Oh? Well now you have to tell me."

"It's kind of a gross job...but if you work with animal guts..."

She wrinkled her nose. "That's an awful way to put it."

"Sorry, god, I'm bad at this." He barked a nervous laugh. "Sanitation, I work in city sanitation."

Annika nodded. "Well, I guess someone has to do it, right?" she asked, echoing what he'd said about her.

"It's not glamorous, but it pays the bills."

"I don't know, I'd say it's one of the most important jobs out there." She imagined what life would be like without people to take away the garbage. Would everyone just go to the dump? Likely things would just end up everywhere. She shuddered. "I don't think the human race will ever be ready to get rid of their own waste."

"Thank you," he said, a hint of surprise lacing his words.

"It's pretty nasty that you've been laughed at for your job." She shook her head sharply.

"Can I ask another question?"

A smirk played her lips. She loved it when a man asked permission. "Yes."

"What's your favourite drink?"

Annika tongued the inside of her cheek. She knew where this was going. Did she want to take a chance on Jon? He seemed sweet, attentive. Could be something to explore.

But Ben's light green eyes flitted through her mind, smacking her with a wave of heat she hadn't felt in a long time. Was her chemistry with him just because they'd seen each other? Because she'd felt the power in his arm beneath her hand? Because he'd been tending to her all night?

"I'm not exactly the alcohol type," she finally said.

"Well…" Jon dragged out the word a little. "I'm going to go hang at the bar. I'll get two virgin cocktails, and if you want to join me, you're welcome to one of them. No pressure."

Annika smiled in the dim light. "Thank you."

"Great, maybe I'll see you later!" There was that nervous energy, that edge to his voice. He was hopeful.

She didn't say anything, and he didn't continue talking, so

after a time she assumed that he was gone. She checked her phone. Fifteen minutes left of the event. She had a few missed messages from her group chat with Gianna and Taylor, the latter sending rundowns of her horrific dates.

Gianna: OMG who even leads with that?

Taylor: Right? Guy legit seemed PROUD he was here to cheat on his wife. This has been the worst crop of dudes ever at one of these!! I hope Annie is doing better than me.

Annika chuckled as she caught up on the conversation, but then her stomach flipped.

Taylor: Security boy is a 10/10 tho damn

A wave of possessiveness rolled through her like a tsunami, as much as she willed it to go away. She didn't have any sort of claim on Ben. He'd done his little intro with each of the women here, it's not like he was taking care of her because he wanted *her*.

She found herself circling the button again, drawing the pad of her finger around the smooth plastic. He was just her type of gorgeous. He'd seemed into her. Then again, so had Jon, and he was actually here tonight for the purpose of dating.

Fuck it, she thought, and pushed the button. *Taking a chance, it's always worth taking a chance.*

The door behind her opened. "Are you alright?"

The voice was alien, and Annika startled, whirling around in her seat. "Oh, yes, I must have accidentally hit the button," she stammered. Before she could stop herself, she blurted, "Where's Ben?"

"He took off early."

Her heart sank. Had she scared him away? "Oh." The word slipped out, her voice near petulant.

"You sure you're okay?" the new guy asked.

Annika nodded jerkily. "Yeah, thank you, sorry for the trouble."

"No problem," he replied with a smile, and shut the door.

She let out a deep sigh, a hand rising to her mouth as it always did when she was extra pensive. She'd been so sure they had chemistry, even if she hadn't pegged him as being compatible with her particular kinks. Clearly she'd come on too strong, though. Disappointment panged in her gut, but she also just felt horrible that she'd freaked him out. She wasn't in the business of making men uncomfortable...unless they wanted her to, of course.

She ran her fingernail across her lower lip. *Well, I guess this is fate's way of telling me that Jon is the one to take a chance on,* she thought, and reached for her purse.

"Hello there, ma'am," a familiar voice came through the booth, the words caressing her skin like silk. "I'm Ben. What's your name?"

Chapter Three

OH MY GOD, ANNIKA THOUGHT, HER HEART RACING. "Are you...did you..." she stammered, unable to find the right words.

"You sounded disappointed that I left," Ben said, his voice clear through whatever speaker that linked the booths together. "Apologies, I was hoping that you wouldn't find me gone before I could get in here."

She crossed her arms, suddenly unsure of what to do with her limbs. "I *was* disappointed...but now, this is like...this is really cute." She couldn't help but admit this, not only to him but to herself. She'd convinced herself to give him a chance, then had the gut punch that he had left because she'd come on too strong, but now it turned out he was interested enough to slip out of work and surprise her in here?

"You pushed the security button," he finally said.

She flushed, her chest growing hot. If he'd heard her exchange with the other bouncer, then yeah, he knew she'd pushed the button, looking for him. *Own it, own the shit out of it, girl.* "Sure did."

They sat in silence for a moment, but it wasn't uncomfortable. It felt like—like they were really getting to know each other. Feeling one another out. This was backwards to how the event was supposed to go. The point was to get to know one another not based on looks, but on conversation, and then see each other after.

But she'd seen Ben, appraised his gorgeousness already, they'd exchanged banter, she'd decided she wanted to fuck him and now...now what were they supposed to do here? Start over?

"And you...left your post to talk to me through a curtain," she finally said, and realized that her hand had risen up to rest on her chest, a tell that she was feeling wholly affected by this man.

His soft chuckle was like a massage, her muscles relaxing beneath the sound.

"I'm not normally so impulsive," he admitted. "I just didn't want to miss my chance. I figured it wasn't a fair go if I didn't get in the booth with your string of other suitors."

She snorted. "Suitors." She wondered what he looked like, sitting in there, what position he was in. Was he seated comfortably in the chair, or was he leaning forward apprehensively? Was he standing, hands clasped in front of him, like he'd been when he was in the hallway? A thrill ran through her at how close she'd become with his body language in such a short time, that she missed reading it already.

"I suppose you should tell me your name, ma'am," Ben said, and she could hear the wry smile in his tone. "Since I told you mine."

Brat, she thought, and then shivered delightfully at the thought. "Ma'am is fine," she quipped, and she could have sworn she heard him take in a sharp breath, but it was difficult to tell with the way sound passed through the booths. "What do you do for a living, Ben?"

"I'm an accountant," he replied, which had her brow

furrowing in confusion. But before she could interject, he continued, "And an occasional bouncer. My cousin owns this bar, and when she hosts events like these she calls all the biggest guys she knows to come help out."

Oh, Annika thought, shaking her head. "An accountant, hm?" She rested her hands on the armrests of the plush chair, lightly drumming the fingernails of her right hand. "So you have a big brain to go with your big biceps?"

There was that chuckle again, and her chest twinged. It was endearing, that sound, and she found herself wanting to make him laugh over and over again.

"I suppose so," he said, and she imagined him blushing in the dim light. "I just have a head for numbers."

Imagined his cheeks pinking so sweetly, as his green eyes shone with nervous excitement. *Gah, I need to calm down.* "Don't sell yourself short," she said, and despite her self-talk her voice came out lower and more like a purr than she'd meant it to. "You're also very eloquent."

There was that sharp breath noise again, and now she was sure he would be blushing. She wanted to see him so badly—but was this supposed to escalate so quick? She had to give him the space to get to know her. She'd been afraid she scared him away once, she didn't want to do it for real.

"Thank you, ma'am," he said, voice breathy, and she nearly melted into a puddle in her seat. He cleared his throat, and then asked, clearer this time, "What do *you* do for a living?"

Patience, space, patience and space, she thought, and straightened her shoulders. *Pretend you don't know what he looks like, what his pretty pink cheeks look like, how you fantasized about him on his knees in front of you, looking up with those big green eyes—FOCUS ANNIKA!* "I'm a vet tech," she said, proud of how not-hoarse she sounded.

"Ah, a noble profession," Ben replied, and she imagined

him nodding along. "Doing all the work the vet doesn't want to do, plus overtime, for pennies."

Her heart skipped a beat. "You sound like you have experience," she said. Many people didn't even know what a tech was, they only ever focused on the 'vet' part.

"My mother was a tech for twenty years before she finally had enough saved to go to vet school," he explained. "She wanted to have her own practice someday."

Annika swallowed hard. *Wanted* insinuated that Ben's mother didn't achieve her dream, and she wasn't sure if she should invite him to explain why or not. "Vet school is expensive," she settled on saying. "Many don't get to that point. She must be a dedicated woman."

"She is."

She let out a soft sigh of relief when he said *is* instead of *was*. "So does she enjoy the work, then?" she asked. A horrible small part of her wondered how funny it would be if Ben's mother was her boss. Dr. O'Leary was maybe a little young to have a son his age, and they looked nothing alike, but it would be one of those odd twists of fate, wouldn't it?

"No, she realized that she didn't," he said with an affectionate laugh. "When she was doing her final in-clinic hours for her degree, she asked me to help her with some financial planning for her future business, and I discovered how far in debt she was from footing the bill for so many pets. If someone couldn't pay and couldn't get pet insurance, she would figure it out for them...and I realized why it had taken her twenty years to save up for vet school."

Annika's heart swelled. "That is...that is so sweet." Her hand was back on her chest again, imagining a soft green-eyed lady staunchly telling a grieving family that they didn't have to worry about their sick pet. How many times had she been in a situation like that? How many times had she done her best to try to work something out for a pet owner that couldn't afford something expensive? Dr. O'Leary did a lot of quiet pro-bono work in emergencies too, though she didn't advertise it for fear of people taking advantage. "So, she didn't end up having enough for her own clinic?"

"She runs a no-kill shelter instead," Ben explained, and the adoration in his voice turned her chest to goo. "Once she got her finances figured out, one of the local humane societies was liquidating its assets and shutting down. She managed to get it for a really good price, and turned it into a sort of adoption center."

Annika leaned forward. "Wait, is Sadie your mom?" Her eyes lit up. "She's a legend in the animal community! I've sent a lot of people her way for adoptions. Our clinic helped the high school do a fundraiser for her last summer, it was so much fun. She is so lovely."

"That she is," he said.

How did our flirting turn into this guy gushing over how awesome his mom is? He's so fucking cute. "Here I was worried that your mom might be my boss or something, and it turns out I know her after all." She laughed, shaking her head. "Small world."

"I hope that's not weird for you," he said, his voice straining a little. "That you know my mother professionally."

Annika cocked a brow, the corner of her mouth curling a touch. "And why would it be weird?" she asked, injecting as much innocence into her voice as possible. "Are you harbouring *unprofessional* thoughts?"

Third time was the charm—his sharp little gasp-breath was louder this time, and she'd been waiting for it. She wanted to see his face so badly, but couldn't deny she was also very much enjoying the buildup.

"I wouldn't want to be disrespectful, ma'am," he said.

She bit down hard on her lower lip. *Oh, sweetie, what a good answer that is.*

Chapter Four

"I find that an excellent trait in a person," Annika said, struggling to keep the heat out of her tone. *Patience, patience, but fuck he's calling me ma'am and talking about respect and—*

"I got that impression from you," Ben said.

She wasn't sure what to do with that, so she filed it away for later. "And what do you look for in a potential partner?" If they were treating this like a getting-to-know-you-so-we-can-maybe-date, then she was going to go all in. She was itching to run her fingers through his hair, nuzzle against the stubble along his jaw, see how *respectful* he really could be—

"Assertiveness…confidence." He sounded hesitant, almost shy. As if saying those very words out loud obliterated his own.

She'd seen him assertive and confident. Mister security man, standing guard to protect the ladies. He'd even taken the initiative to slip into the booth to impress her. But now that he was here, on the spot, his nerves were showing, and she couldn't help but find that endearing.

"I bet you get a lot of that in the workplace," she said casually. "From the higher-ups."

She could almost hear the smirk in his voice as he replied, "I *am* the higher-ups. I spend most of my day managing junior accountants."

"Interesting," she said, before she could stop herself.

Ben chuckled. "What, that I spend all day in charge, and just don't want to anymore by the end of it?"

Annika struggled with how to answer this. She understood. In her day job, she was the vet's go-get-it girl. It wasn't the specific cause of her penchant for dominance, but it definitely made it that much sweeter when she was alone at the end of the day to fantasize.

She couldn't help but feel like she'd found a kindred spirit in Ben, but was too afraid to say so. That definitely seemed to cross the line in coming on too strong, even though her kink senses were going haywire. She wanted to make sure that he was comfortable, safe, and fully consenting.

She was past the point now where she could just pretend. This man was bringing out her inner domme in a thrilling way, and she didn't think she could be intimate with him and hold it back.

It also surprised her that, no matter how long she took to speak, he didn't prompt her. Their thoughtful silences were comfortable, and he was giving her the space she needed to contemplate. She liked that in a companion--no pressure to endlessly chatter and fill the quiet.

"Yes," she finally said, short and sweet without elaboration.

"May I ask a question, ma'am?"

So damn polite, she thought, heart fluttering. "You may."

"I would really like to ask you out." He paused briefly. "But I understand we've met under...unconventional circumstances. And I'm unsure of how to proceed here. If I should ask to open the curtains, even though we've already met face-to-face. If I should ask you to go for a drink at the bar, risking my cousin teasing me like crazy for ducking out early to court a woman—"

"Court me?" Annika cut in, shaking her head and stifling a snort. "How about I save you all this uncertainty, because I prefer to be the one to do the *courting*, okay?"

Ben let out a deep breath.

She raised her chin, mustering all of her courage. "I'd like you to walk me home. When we get there, you can decide whether you'd like to come up and spend time with me, or exchange numbers and spend time together another day." She needed to be out in the world with him, away from his job, away from this event. Just the two of them, chatting in the freedom of the night air, being able to look at each other—touch each other.

She wanted to run a hand through his silky-looking hair and ask him, while staring deep into his eyes, if he wanted her to take him upstairs and take care of him. She could imagine the look on his face and she wanted it to be real, wanted to will it into existence.

"I would love that," he breathed.

She grinned wildly, unable to stop it, her cheeks near painful with her happiness. "Okay then," she said, practically scrambling to her feet. "Open the curtain, sweetheart."

She wondered if he'd leapt up from the chair as well, because the *snick* of the curtain opening was near immediate. This was silly, maybe, since they'd already seen each other's faces, already been within proximity in the hallway. She'd felt the heat radiating from his silky-looking skin.

But she drew out the moment anyway, gently taking the edge of the curtain in her hand and pulling it slowly, revealing the glass between them.

Her breath left her body as their eyes met.

Ben didn't look like he had in the hall. He didn't look like Security Boy anymore. He was a man that had bared himself to her, the vulnerability showing on his face as he gazed through the glass, staring at her as if she were some kind of goddess. She'd thought she could imagine that expression, thought it would take time to bring it out in him, but as it turned out, her imagination couldn't hold a candle to this.

Annika thought maybe, just maybe, her will could do just about damn anything.

Chapter Five

ANNIKA SLIPPED OUT OF HER BOOTH, LOOKING BOTH ways down the hallway. She wanted to make a quick escape without her friends stopping her and potentially grilling Ben. She wanted him all to herself while they got to know each other. She loved her friends, but them half drunk and overbearing in a bar could be...well, it could ruin the vibe she had going.

She checked the group chat, where Taylor and Gianna's last messages had been them coordinating where to meet up in the pub. So they weren't in the booths anymore.

Heading out with someone cute, Annika typed out. *Cross your fingers for me.*

Taylor: OMG so jealous! But happy for you too! Get him girl!

Annika grinned. When they inevitably found out it was the hot security guy Taylor would be even more jealous. She cocked a brow and then added, *Also, there is a very sweet dude named Jon at the bar. He deserves a cute girl to brighten his night.*

Taylor: I'm cute and a girl!

Gianna: And she's on a mission. I hope she doesn't scare him too bad lol. Enjoy your night Annika.

She chuckled and sent back a quick, *Night xox*, and pocketed her phone. As if on cue, Ben emerged from a door at the other end of the hall, waving her down.

The new security guard gave her a little nod as she walked by, and she returned it with a smile before focusing on Ben. He'd said he knew a way out the back that would bypass the pub, which worked out nicely for both of them. She'd wanted to avoid running into Gianna and Taylor, and he didn't want to have to deal with his cousin's ribbing either—especially when he'd taken off early.

Part of Annika wanted to see him squirm a bit under his cousin's teasing, but a bigger part of her was eager to get to their walk. And keep all the teasing for herself.

When she reached him, he lifted one of those muscular arms, and she slid her hand into the crook of his elbow.

"Such a gentleman," she commended, giving him a playful smile.

He winked at her. "Of course, ma'am." His voice was a bit too breathy, a bit excited, despite his best efforts to hide it, and she couldn't help the swell of pride that she'd elicited such a response in him.

"I feel like a celebrity or something, being escorted out the back by security," Annika joked, and he chuckled low in his throat.

"Avoiding throngs of adoring fans," he added as they emerged into a parking lot.

She barked a laugh. "You know, that must be so stressful. I wouldn't want that job."

"Celebrity or security?" He cocked a brow.

She thought for a moment as she led him to the left

towards the road towards her place. "Either," she admitted. "I wouldn't want to have to worry about the world scrutinizing everything I do, nor be responsible for protecting someone else from that."

"Agreed," Ben replied.

"Yet here you are, working security," she teased, poking him in the side with her free hand.

He flinched his muscular body away from her finger and laughed. "Bouncing a pub event is hardly security," he said. "And honestly, I've never actually had to *bounce* anyone. We're really just there to look intimidating and people behave themselves."

"Most of the time," Annika countered. "Though I suppose the sleazy dude with his junk out got bounced by someone else."

"Ah, yeah," Ben said sheepishly. "Mark took care of that guy. I'm sorry you had to deal with that."

She squeezed his arm reassuringly. "Not your fault. Assholes show up everywhere. I appreciate you dealing with it as quickly as you did so he couldn't cause any trouble for anyone else." When they reached the sidewalk, she turned right. The streets weren't exactly crawling with people, but it was a fairly normal weekend night, all the hustle and bustle of revelers enjoying their freedom. People on the prowl for a party or sex or both.

"So, what's your favourite food?" Ben asked, waving his free hand to motion vaguely to all of the various food establishments along the street. Mixed in with the bars and clubs and pubs were all kinds of little speciality restaurants, focused on either one type of food or regional specific.

Annika grinned. "Sushi. Can't get enough."

He scratched the back of his head nervously. "I, ah, I've never had it," he admitted.

"Never had *sushi*?" She gasped, pressing a hand to her

chest to really amp up the mock horror. "I'm offended on behalf of your tastebuds."

He laughed. "I've just never gotten around to it...I'm sure it's delicious, just the raw fish thing squicks me out a bit."

She nodded. "Don't worry, that puts off a lot of people, it's totally normal," she assured him. "Eating food prepared by a restaurant is always a risk though, whether it's raw fish or pizza. You don't know what people are doing or not doing. If you're ever interested in trying it, though, I can personally vet the place near my apartment. They make everything right in front of you, and I've been eating there for three years and have never gotten sick." She took a deep wistful breath. "You're missing out. The taste of raw tuna, my *god* it's so good." A soft moan escaped her lips, and by the hitch in his chest she wondered if he was excited about more than sushi. "What's your favourite food?"

He cleared his throat, his cheeks a little pink, and she couldn't help the sadistic pleasure coursing through her at distracting him in such a way.

"Beef Stroganoff," he replied. "My mom used to make it every Sunday when I was a kid, old family recipe. I'll eat any strog, but that one is just..." He made a chef's kiss motion.

Annika laughed. "Sounds delicious. Now I know where to go for the best stroganoff, then." She imagined him standing over a stove, expertly fussing over sizzling pots and pans, muscles in his forearms working, a focused expression on his face... She blinked at herself with surprise. Here she was fantasizing about Ben, but in a wholly domestic way. And while there were definitely sensual undertones, it was more with a sense of longing to see him doing something he enjoyed.

This was new for her. It was frightening. But the good kind of frightening, like the thrill from riding a roller coaster.

"Happy to cook for you anytime, ma'am," he said with a warm smile, and her chest tightened.

Terrifying. Terrifying that it wasn't just her libido tightening.

"May I ask a question?" He led her around a boisterous group of young men that looked barely old enough to drink, before one of them could barrel into her.

Annika was used to sidestepping random drunk people on the street near her apartment, but she'd been so distracted by all that was Ben that she likely would have smacked right into them. It was a heady feeling, wanting to take the lead but also trusting him to look out for her.

"You may," she replied, forcing her voice to come out smooth.

"You said when we first met that your friends talked you into coming to the dating event," he said slowly, as if he were choosing his words carefully. "Is that because...you didn't want to do the event? Or you're not interested in dating in general?"

The words came out so tentative, so gentle. With the slightly higher pitch, she could tell that he didn't want to sound like he was as invested in the answer as he was.

She took a deep breath, contemplating how she wanted to word her answer. They were only a block away from her apartment now, and she wanted to get it all out on the table before he made the final decision to join her.

"I haven't been interested in dating for a long time, but not particularly because I am opposed to it in general," she said. "I think you've picked up on the fact that I like to be in charge. Most men are not into that. So it makes relations very difficult for me. I tried to just pretend otherwise throughout my twenties, but at this point in my life I'm tired of pretending. I'm thirty-two years old and I've felt pretty resigned to the fact that I might never find someone that I fit with." She let that marinate for a moment, resisting the urge to look up at him to see what his expression looked like.

He hadn't torn his arm away from her, nor had he stiffened or tensed or slowed his pace. They were still leisurely strolling, comfortably so. She took that as a good sign.

"So, I suppose the answer to your question is that I am not *not interested* in dating," Annika continued. "I'm just not interested in being with anyone that I can't be fully myself with."

He didn't answer right away. But it was that amicable silence, that comfortable quiet that had stretched between them in the booths, a mutual respect to let each other think on all angles.

"I am quite certain that I...complement your proclivities," Ben finally said.

She couldn't help the laugh that bubbled up in her throat. "So formal."

His cheeks flushed, and she wanted so badly to kiss them, take them in her hands, he was so damn adorable.

"My only concern is that I've never...explored the part of me that *I've* always had to hide," he continued, his blush deepening and his voice lowering a little.

Annika realized they'd reached her building, and pulled him to a stop. She understood what he was so eloquently saying. He wanted her to take control of him, wanted to submit to her, but he'd never done it before.

She turned to face him, letting go of his arm so she could flatten her palms against his chest. "You'll never have to hide with me," she said, her voice firm. "Never have to pretend to be someone you're not."

How badly had she always wanted someone to say that to her? It felt cathartic to declare it to somebody else, especially as she could feel his body softening beneath her, as if he were melting beneath her hands. It made her feel powerful, and that frightening thrill ripped up her spine like lightning. The relief in his eyes told her he felt seen—accepted. And in turn that made her feel the same way.

"Would you like to come upstairs, Ben?" she asked.

He smiled, a bright grin that lit up the night, and said, "Yes, ma'am."

Chapter Six

Annika led the way up to her apartment, glad that she had taken the time to tidy that morning. It was fully possible that Westley had messed up a bunch of her stuff while she was gone, but she didn't think that Ben would judge her for that. Cats were jerks, adorable little jerks—it couldn't be helped.

She opened the door and gestured Ben into the modest front hall, and he immediately stepped aside upon entering to let her go past. As she locked up, he bowed slightly and raised his hands in an offer to take her coat. She smiled and nodded, shrugging out of the light material so he could take it from her shoulders, hanging it up on one of the nearby hooks. He wasn't wearing a jacket, but slipped off his shoes and lined them up neatly next to her heels on the little mat next to the door.

Annika led the way through the small space. It was an upgrade from the tiny studio apartment she'd lived in before—at least this place had a bedroom separate from the living room and kitchen area. She ushered him towards the love seat in the living room, her tiny couch just right for one person—or two, if they wanted to squish up next to each other.

Which, she did, very much, want to squish up against Ben. She wanted to do a lot up against him.

He settled into the couch, and almost immediately Westley jumped into his lap with an offended *prrrowww*.

Annika laughed, shaking her head. "Sorry about that," she said. "He likes to command a room."

"Just like his momma," Ben cooed as he snuggled the fat black cat, rubbing affectionately behind his ears.

Her chest warmed as she watched him turn to putty over Westley, and she nestled into the couch, watching her sweet cat purr and love all over her guest. Westley was a friendly cat as it was, but he didn't often lavish strangers with so much attention. Not that she had a lot of strangers in her home, but he hadn't been like this when Gianna or Taylor had visited for the first time.

"He likes you," Annika said, and Ben glanced up at her with a soft expression, a sweetness in his eyes that melted her.

"I like him too," he replied, chuckling as his hand paused and Westley bonked his forehead against it impatiently.

After a sufficient rub down, the cat jumped down, tail flicking back and forth as he went in search of his food bowl.

"Would you like something to drink?" Annika offered, inclining her head towards the kitchen.

Ben shook his head. "No ma'am, thank you," he said. "I'm happy to get you something though, if you direct me."

Her lip curled into a small smile. She hadn't particularly wanted anything, but she loved that he'd offered and wanted to see how he did.

"I was thinking of tea," she mused. "How are you at making tea?"

He grinned. "Bagged or loose leaf?"

Promising answer, she thought. "Loose leaf," she replied.

"You can find everything you need in the cupboard next to the fridge."

He got up, and there was something in his gait, something different than before. He didn't have that same hard-edge security vibe going on, but it wasn't as if he'd withered, either. He had a confidence about him, but this air of submissiveness that drove his movements. Thankfully her kitchen was open-concept, so she could watch him move around, his muscular frame rippling beneath his clothes.

I can't wait to get you out of those, she thought, drawing her lower lip between her teeth as he pulled items from the cupboard, lining everything up in a neat little row on the counter.

He moved almost like a dancer, so graceful as he filled the kettle, setting it on the stove to boil as he scooped two tablespoons of Earl Grey tea into her infuser mug and promptly resealed the tin. He replaced the items he was finished with to the cupboard, then seemed to notice the honey jar in there. He pulled it out, turning slightly to hold it up, his eyebrow raised in question.

"Just a dollop, please," Annika said, licking her lips as he nodded and popped open the jar with ease, the muscles in his forearm twitching with the motion.

He shifted his weight to one hip, giving her a lovely view of his taut ass muscles on that side as he waited for the kettle to boil. As soon as it whistled, he turned off the oven and poured the steaming water in a slow circular motion over the infuser, filling the mug to the brim. He gently set the ceramic topper over the mug, and then fished his phone out of his pocket. He swiped and tapped a few times, and before Annika could inquire why he was texting someone in the middle of his task, he held up the screen to show her he'd set a three-minute timer.

She chuckled. "You're very good at this," she called, and

extended her legs so that her feet rested on the coffee table, crossed at the ankles.

"My mom is a tea addict," he explained. "I was taught at a young age how to properly prepare all kinds. Or at least, how she likes them. I hope three minutes is okay for you?"

"Absolutely," Annika replied. "I don't use a timer, but that sounds about right for how much I like it steeped."

He winked. "I'm very thorough."

"We'll see," she teased, and he cocked a brow as if accepting a challenge.

When the timer went off, Ben lifted the infuser and gently wiggled it before setting it in the sink and adding a perfect dollop of honey to the tea. He stirred it, then brought the mug back to the couch with expert grace, not appearing to move carefully but also not spilling a single drop.

He held out the mug to Annika, and she took it with a nod of thanks, blowing some of the steam from the top and then taking a deep whiff of bergamot.

Before she could take a sip, he patted his thigh and motioned to her feet. "May I?"

She licked her lips and shifted sideways so that her legs were across his lap. She was short enough that even on the two-seater couch, they could both comfortably face each other while he took a hold of her foot and began massaging.

Annika let out a deep sigh of relief, and took a tentative sip of her hot tea. The sweetness of the honey perfectly melded with the bite of the Earl Grey, a lovely balm that complemented the relaxing movements of Ben's digits against her tired foot. She felt like a queen, a goddess.

"I could get used to this," she joked, and though he smiled there was something else in his eyes, a longing that plucked at her heartstrings. When he didn't say anything, she prompted, "Tell me what you're thinking about."

A cute blush crept up his cheeks, and he lowered his gaze

to his work, watching his fingers manipulating the arch of her foot. "Just thinking I could get used to this, too." His blush deepened.

"Don't be embarrassed of what you want," Annika said, and though not loud, her voice was firm. "Even if it is cute as hell when you blush."

His face screwed up, an it looked like he was trying hard not to smile, his cheeks growing even redder. "Nobody has ever called me *cute* before."

"I find that really hard to believe." She cocked a brow, taking another sip of her delicious drink.

He shook his head.

"Well, maybe not that you've *heard*," she insisted. "But I'd bet money that many women have called you cute in private."

He chuckled nervously. "If it's out of earshot it doesn't count," he said. "How is your tea?"

She smiled. "Heavenly, thank you." She inclined her head. "As are your hands. Are you going to tell me you learned how to do foot massages from Sadie, too?"

A laugh burst out of him, short and loud. "No, no," he said, shaking his head vehemently. "I'm learning as I go here." His touch turned more tentative as he said the words.

"Hey, what did I say about embarrassment?" Annika asked, raising her chin. "You're doing wonderfully. If you need guidance, I'll guide you. You don't have to be afraid. Just be you."

Ben raised his gaze, depths of emotions flitting across his features at her words. He didn't say anything for a long while, the two of them staring at each other as he continued massaging her, deeper and with more confidence this time. Eventually, he switched to the other foot, and Annika sighed happily, taking another sip of her warm tea, her body melting into the couch cushions.

"You're beautiful," he finally said, the sudden noise startling her from her comfortable reverie.

Now it was Annika's turn to have warm cheeks. She'd never lacked confidence in her appearance. Though not as conventionally-shaped as her best friends, she knew she was attractive and enjoyed her body. But it was still a nice thing to hear, especially from such a sweet and alluring man.

"Thank you," she said. "So are you."

"From the second you opened up that booth, I..." He shook his head. "You surprised me. Is it awful of me that I kept hoping you'd meet incompatible men so you'd keep coming back into the hallway?"

She laughed, shaking her head. "If it is, then I'm also awful, because I spent most of my time in there trying to stop myself from pushing the security button and totally abuse your job posting to talk to you."

"You *did* end up pushing it, though," he reminded her.

She shrugged, and eyed him over the rim of her mug. "I guess I'm awful, then."

"You're the furthest thing from awful," he breathed, and his hands stopped massaging as he shook his head slowly. "You're..." He trailed off, his mouth opening and closing, as if he struggled to find the right words.

Annika took pity on him and set her mug down on the coffee table. "I didn't think such an eloquent man could ever be caught speechless," she teased.

"It's very rare," he admitted sheepishly.

A wicked gleam sparkled in her eyes. "Well, then I think I have a better use for that mouth."

Chapter Seven

Annika couldn't help but stare at Ben's luscious mouth. She had so many ideas for how he could use it. Too many. The heat in his gaze was palpable, coupled with a sweet vulnerability that made her want to protect him, wrap him up and never let him go. She knew she was past the point of no return, now. They were no longer teetering on the edge—they'd plunged into the deep end and the water felt mighty fine.

She gently curled her legs beneath her. "Before we continue, I want you to know that if you're uncomfortable at any time you let me know and I will stop immediately. Don't be shy or second-guess, communicate with me, understood?"

He nodded firmly. "That goes for you as well, ma'am. Please let me know if you need to stop for any reason."

She smiled, warmth blooming in her chest. "Thank you." She hadn't thought about it, but it was nice to know that he had her best interests and consent in his mind too. She got to her feet. "Come to the bedroom." She led the way, entering the minimalist room and sitting down on the edge of her plush queen-sized bed.

He stood before her, his massive frame towering over her, and she quivered with the power over this beautiful man. He was so big and strong and willing to bend for her and she felt drunk on it.

"Kneel," she said, and though it was a command, her voice stayed gentle, like a silken caress.

Ben sank to his knees in front of her without hesitation, his face slightly upturned now that his eye-level was at the height of her collarbone. His bottom lip disappeared into his mouth for a split second, his eyes lingering on her mouth.

"Are you thinking about kissing me?" she asked.

He took in a breath, that sweet sharp little inhale she was coming to love. That sign that he was disarmed, caught, excited.

"Tell me," she prompted. "Tell me what you're thinking about."

"I'm imagining what your lips feel like," he said hoarsely. "What you taste like." He swallowed hard. "Ma'am."

She reached out, brushing her fingers against his cheek, sliding them across his skin and around the back, threading into his hair. His eyes fluttered closed and he leaned into the touch.

"So polite," she cooed. "So sweet." She drew her hand back down his cheek to his jaw, cupping his face. "If you want to kiss me, just ask."

He opened his beautiful eyes and stared up at her with a magnetism that nearly pulled her from sheer longing alone. "May I kiss you, ma'am?" he breathed.

"Yes, you may," she whispered, and she thought he would launch himself at her, close the distance before she could even blink.

But it appeared this man had amazing self control. He drew out the moment, leaning in slowly, his eyes flicking down to her waiting mouth. He brought his own hands up, taking her cheeks in his massive palms, his long eyelashes fluttering again as he got closer and closer.

Then his lips were on hers, and they gasped in unison, stealing each other's breath, and Annika felt weightless. It was so tentative but so sensual, the way his mouth massaged hers, as if he were savouring her, drinking every mewl that reverberated in her throat. She slid her fingers up the back of his neck, deepening the kiss, swallowing his helpless moan. That noise drove her libido into overdrive. The fact that she had this gorgeous man completely at her mercy, able to draw such a needy sound from him with a kiss alone…

She finally pulled away, the need to breathe desperate, their chests heaving as they parted. They stared at each other for a moment, and then Annika licked her swollen lips.

"Was it what you imagined?" she asked hoarsely.

"Better, ma'am," he whispered.

She ran a finger down his chest, dancing along the waistband of his jeans. There was a sizable bulge below, but she wasn't ready for that yet. There was much more squirming to be had, first.

"Take off your shirt," she instructed, tugging on the thin fabric.

He hooked his fingers below the bottom hem and drew the garment up over his sculpted abdomen slowly, revealing his luscious skin inch by agonizing inch. When he pulled the t-shirt free of his face, he met her gaze with a fire that promised her he was, indeed, squirming.

"I want you to undress me," she said, and then held up a perfectly-manicured finger, "without using your hands."

Ben's lower lip disappeared again, and he let it go with a soft *pop*. He raised his palms up as if in surrender, and then made a show of lowering them and putting them behind his back. The position shifted the muscles in his chest, stretching his shoulders taut, and she purred appreciatively at the submissive pose.

He leaned forward, nuzzling his face against her knee as he made his way up her thigh. She knew she'd given him a challenge—her skirt had a zipper on the side that was near invisible. He moved towards it, though, and she wondered how often he'd been checking her out that evening to know the ins and outs of her clothes in the dim light. That thought warmed her even further, the thought that he'd been thinking about this just as long as she had.

He leaned right over, taking the zipper between his teeth, giving her an excellent view of his strong arms crossed behind his back. His hands clenched into fists as he attempted to work the zipper, slipping once or twice but finally managing to get it all the way down. He took one side of the open flap in his mouth and gently tugged, and Annika lifted a little so he could bring the skirt out from under her.

Once it was free, she sat back down and watched him pull it down her legs where the fabric pooled at her ankles. Seeing him like that, shirtless and bent right over, his thighs and abs doing the work with his ass in the air as he freed her skirt from each leg in turn...she thought she was going to spontaneously combust. She was so close to just tearing their clothes off right there, but god, the anticipation was so delicious, too.

And she wanted to see how he made out with the rest of her clothes. Her top was an asymmetrical off-the-shoulder cut, fairly loose on her, and he opted to take the bottom hem in his teeth and slowly rise to his feet. She giggled as the shirt caught on her face, and wriggled her arms a bit to help him get it up and over her.

He stood there for a beat, her shirt still hanging from his mouth, as his eyes roved over her lingerie-clad body. All black lace, her nipples peeking out through the flowery pattern, full breasts heavy and desperate to be free.

He tossed the shirt aside with the skirt, and then made his way around the side of the bed to kneel behind her on the mattress. It took him three tries to bite her bra clasp in just the right way to open it, and Annika arched her back.

Ben scrambled around to the floor again, kneeling before her. He ghosted his lips over the top of one pillowy breast before the other, making her shiver, and then kissed her flesh, lips half over her skin and half over the lace of the cup.

She grasped his hair, tugging gently. "Don't get distracted, now," she said breathlessly. "Be a good boy and take it off."

He groaned with need against her, leaning his face into her chest for a moment as if to collect himself before taking her bra in his teeth and pulling back. She straightened her arms so he could pull the garment free, and then dropped it, staring at her hungrily.

Annika raised one leg and rested it on his strong shoulder. "Only one left," she said, "and then we'll put that mouth to good use."

Chapter Eight

As Ben drew Annika's panties down her thighs with his teeth, he held her gaze, and it was as if time slowed down. He moved slowly, his warm breath puffing on her sensitive flesh, and the pure heat in his eyes threatened to melt her completely. Once the garment was finally free, he didn't toss it aside, didn't break his submission and leap on her.

He sat back on his haunches, hands still behind his back, holding the lace in his mouth and staring at her with questioning need. He was waiting for instructions.

She chewed her bottom lip for a moment as she regarded him. She could hardly contain herself, but she wanted to make him sweat, make him wait, make him *want.* He was doing so well, being so obedient, and she wanted him inside of her so badly but she also never wanted this to end.

So she spread her knees, and leaned back on her hands, giving him a perfect view of her. "Would you like to taste me?"

His lips parted, and the panties fell to the floor as he gazed at her. He seemed to struggle to find his voice as he roved his eyes over her waiting body, and then he shut his mouth and swallowed hard.

"Yes..." he said hoarsely, clearing his throat before he added, "ma'am."

She curled a finger to beckon him closer. "Show me your skills then, sweetheart," she purred.

Ben shuffled forward to the edge of the bed, and leaned down to kiss her soft thigh. She wanted to tell him not to tease her, to just get to it, but bit back the words. She wanted him to have the freedom to show her what he could do—she'd instructed him to do just that, and didn't want to limit how he explored her body.

He kept his hands behind his back, though, and she relished that he hadn't moved them because she hadn't told him he could. She decided to leave it that way for now.

He suckled at her flesh gently, working his way towards her drenched pussy. Her clit pulsed with anticipation as he ghosted his breath over the bundle of nerves, and she spread her thighs as far as they could go, presenting herself to his mouth.

And then he was on her, and her head fell back, a throaty sound tearing its way from her throat as she lost herself in the sensations. He explored her with a perfect blend of soft pressure and languid licks. She rolled her hips gently, reaching down with a hand to massage his scalp, every once in awhile drawing her nails along his skin lightly. She didn't want to direct him, only let him know through all of his senses that she was intensely enjoying herself.

Somehow despite only the one part of her body being manipulated by him, it felt like he was in every nerve ending, everywhere, all around her. She wanted him to feel the same way. Like she was all-encompassing.

And then Annika couldn't think anymore, because the pleasure building in her hit a fever pitch, a spring coiling itself tight in her belly, and before she could register it or realize it was about to happen, an orgasm blindsided her. She wailed her pleasure, letting go of his hair to fist the sheets, the muscles in her body tensing as her nerves exploded in euphoria.

He drew out the waves of pleasure, licking her sweetly, drinking every last spasm until she couldn't take the sensation anymore, her flesh so sensitive it was almost painful.

"Enough," she breathed, and he immediately stopped, sinking back onto his haunches, staring up at her with those big viridescent eyes, his chin shining with the proof of her arousal.

Still so obedient, with his hands behind his back.

"Remove your pants," she instructed, her voice shaky and breathless as she recovered from the best orgasm she'd ever had.

He looked down, and then back up at her. "May I use my hands, ma'am?" he asked.

It took Annika a moment to realize what he was asking, her pleasure-addled brain a tick behind. "Oh, yes," she finally said, shaking her head when she realized. "Of course."

Ben's lip curled the slightest bit on the edge, the submissive boy allowing himself a bit of smugness for breaking her brain.

But she didn't call him out on it—he deserved it.

Annika watched him unbutton his jeans, and then get to his feet, shoving his pants and boxers down together. She couldn't even chastise him for doing the boxers too, because she was so distracted by his massive dick that sprung free. Her mouth went dry at the sight of it—she'd assumed by the sizable bulge that he was large, but she hadn't imagined this.

As he stepped out of his garments, she noticed the blush on his cheeks and his downcast eyes.

"Shy boy," she cooed, finally managing to find her voice after all that huffing and moaning. "Look at that magnificent cock."

He blushed even harder, and then followed her instructions, looking down at himself.

"What are you self-conscious about?" she asked.

He shook his head a little, and then raised his gaze to hers. "I don't want to hurt you." He didn't add the *ma'am* this time, and Annika didn't correct him, because he was being so vulnerable with her and she wanted to give him the space to do so.

"Oh, that's not going to happen," she said, and waved for him to come forward. "I am wetter than I've ever been in my life, and I'm going to be in complete control. You don't have to worry about hurting me."

He knelt down again against the edge of the bed, so she wasn't looking up at him anymore. She cupped his cheeks, staring deep into his sparkling green eyes, and curled her legs around his waist to draw their now-naked bodies flush together.

"You don't have to be afraid with me," she whispered. "I'm going to take care of you. Are you okay to let me do that?"

He nodded slowly, something akin to adoration in his eyes. "Yes, ma'am."

Chapter Nine

Annika slithered back on the bed, beckoning Ben forward. He crawled up onto the mattress, and she gently pushed on his chest until he lay on his back, baring his gorgeous body to her. She leaned down, kissing his forehead, then his nose, then his cheekbone. She lingered on his lips for a moment, then kissed his chin.

"You're perfect," she whispered as she kissed along his collarbone. "Fucking perfect."

He quivered beneath her, reaching up and drawing his palms up her back. She straddled the deep v of his sculpted pelvis, sliding her hands up the ridges of his abs. She really couldn't believe his job was to sit at a desk all day with a body like this.

His hands settled on her waist and she drew her fingers up and down his forearms before gently taking his wrists and moving his arms above his head. He gasped as she held them there, his hips rolling beneath her, and she smirked down at him.

"You like being pinned, sweetheart?" she asked, and he nodded, lips parted as his breaths came out in hot pants.

He could so easily overpower her. He could probably lift her with one arm. But he was giving himself to her, letting her hold him down and take control of him. Her pussy clenched around nothing, desperate to swallow his thick cock, and she knew she couldn't hold back much longer. She wanted him so badly.

She didn't want this night to end, and it hit her like a lightning strike how she already wanted him *again* and she hadn't even had him once. Again and again and again...she shoved those thoughts aside. She couldn't get distracted by terrifying needy thoughts like that. She wanted to make this count, live and feel in every single moment, because Ben was giving her every part of himself and she wanted to cherish every bit of it.

She leaned a little so she could reach her nightstand, and rummaged around in the drawer for a foil packet. He reached for it, but she shook her head.

"You keep your hands up there, sweetheart," she instructed. "I've got you."

Those last three words took the breath right out of her as they came out, as she hadn't been expecting them to feel the way they did. Something flickered over Ben's gaze as well, and though she was instantly terrified that it was fear, it was that well of longing she'd caught a glimpse of before. Warmth spread across her chest.

She shimmied her way down his body until his massive cock was in front of her. He swallowed hard, and she watched his face as she wrapped a hand around the shaft, pumping it once. He drew his satiny bottom lip between his teeth, his eyelashes fluttering.

"Don't hold back," Annika instructed. "I want to hear every noise you make."

She applied a bit of pressure in her fist, moving her hand up and down the silky smooth skin, memorizing every ridge and vein with her palm. The sound of pure abandon that tore out of Ben's throat had her letting out her own moan, and she couldn't take it anymore.

She tore open the foil packet and tossed the wrapper aside, positioning the condom on the thick head. It was a stretch to roll it down, and with each movement she imagined the stretch she was going to feel inside.

Ben's breathing quickened as she propped herself up on her knees, positioning her sopping pussy over him.

Annika stared into his eyes intently. "Are you still okay?" she asked, forcing her voice to stay calm. She didn't want to pressure him. She wanted him to know that he was safe with her.

He nodded, his eyes filled with pure molten heat. "Yes," he said hoarsely. "Yes."

She lowered herself down onto him, and they gasped at the same time as his girth parted her slick folds. She flattened her palms against his chest, and let gravity do the work, slowly sheathing his cock with her body.

It was the most delicious stretch she'd ever felt—not quite painful, just that feeling that she was pushing her body to do something important, something that was scary but good. And maybe that didn't even apply to the actual sex itself. Maybe the scary part was something totally different.

"Oh my god, oh my god," Ben moaned, his eyes shut tight, fists clenched. He kept his hands above his head, though, and she admired his self-control because Annika's mind was spinning at the feel of their joining.

When she finally reached the bottom and her thighs and ass settled against his body, neither of them breathed. It was as if time stopped, for how long, she wasn't sure, and then she took in a deep, ragged breath as she got used to the girth inside of her. She gave her hips the tiniest experimental roll and he whimpered, a sound so full of need and lust that she thought she might drown in it.

"Come here," she said, holding out her hands, and he sat up immediately, curling his arms around her back, pulling their chests flush against each other once again.

He bent to kiss her, but he was still so much taller than her even sitting down that it didn't last very long due to the odd angle. They parted breathlessly and he rested his face down on the top of her head.

"Are you okay?" he murmured into her hair, a desperate edge to his voice.

"I'm amazing," she replied, kissing his chest as she rolled her hips again. "You're amazing."

"I've never been...god, I've never been so deep," he moaned, his voice coming out at a higher pitch than before, wavering and gasping as if he were on the edge of insanity.

Annika lightly raked her nails down his back, kissing along his collarbone. She rolled her hips again, and this time didn't stop, beginning a gentle rocking motion. The ridges of his throbbing cock massaged her inner walls deliciously, and she could already feel a storm building. The feel of him being everywhere, touching fucking *everywhere*, was back in full force, a completeness that felt like they'd been joined as one.

He groaned against her, clutching her as if she were the only thing anchoring him to the earth.

They moved together at that slow, languid pace, for an indeterminate amount of time. It could have been hours or minutes, Annika was so lost in every sensation, every ebb and flow of their lovemaking. Ben leaned her back so he could bend to kiss her, their mouths crashing together, and she exploded, groaning her release into his mouth, unable to contain the euphony of every one of her nerves singing at the same time.

His mouth tasted like her still, her musk an echo on his tongue, and he kissed her deeply as she came down from her high, her body melting.

She slid her hands up to cup his jaw, gently parting their faces so she could breathe. For two of the most intense orgasms of her life, she wanted to make sure that he had an out-of-body experience for his.

"Don't move," she instructed, and reached around him to pile pillows beneath his back. She pushed him gently down atop them, so he was comfortable but elevated enough that he would have a good show. She took his hands in hers, interlacing their fingers, keeping her hips steady, unmoving, just holding them joined.

She could tell by his short breaths and the desperation in his eyes that he wanted to move. He wanted to thrust. Wanted to touch.

"You're such a good boy," she said, and his cock twitched inside of her, his lips parting in a soft moan. "Good boys get rewarded."

She braced her knees on either side of him and lifted her hips. She knew that she wouldn't be able to get as far up his shaft as she would have liked because of his length, but even being able to get halfway should be able to give him the sensations that she wanted to elicit. Once she was there, she let herself fall back against him, a lot quicker this time than the first with the extra lubrication and her having adjusted to his size.

His eyes fluttered closed and he let out a guttural groan, his jaw tightening.

So she did it again.

And again.

Annika sped up her pace, holding his hands, using her thigh muscles to jackhammer herself down onto him, the wet slaps of the frantic movement echoing in time with his moaning breaths. Another orgasm built in her like a storm, but she refused to let it whirl until he was in the throes of his, refused to let it take over.

"I—may I—" Ben gasped, seemingly unable to make a proper sentence, but she knew what he was asking.

"Yes," she breathed, "let go—"

Before she could even finish the word, he cried out, his body tensing, and she buried him to the hilt, finally giving in to her own pleasure, squeezing his hands as if they were sharing electricity back and forth between their bodies. Her vision dimmed at the edges with the force of it, pleasure sending her muscles into a frenzy, and when it let her free she collapsed forward in the aftershocks.

Ben caught her, disentangling their hands just in time to fold her limp body against his, and they snuggled into each other, nothing but a sweaty mass of heaving chests and afterglow.

Annika couldn't tell where her body ended and his began, their limbs fitting together so perfectly, and there was nowhere else in the world that she would rather be.

He stared at her with something akin to awe in his gaze, a deep vulnerability swirling with adoration.

She held him tightly. *I've got you.*

Chapter Ten

THE AIR IN THE ROOM FELT THICK, NOT unpleasantly so, just heavy with something that felt important. Annika wasn't sure how to purely address it, wasn't sure how to bring it up, wasn't sure exactly how to articulate anything. The feelings swelling in her chest threatened to spill over, and even now, even with the adoration in Ben's gaze as he lightly stroked his fingers up and down her arm, she was afraid she would scare him away.

First she'd been scared to tell him about her kinky proclivities, and now that that had worked out and was out of the way, she was afraid to tell him how much this night had meant to her. They'd known each other for five minutes...but somehow it felt like longer, it felt like a millennia.

"Tell me what you're thinking about?" His voice was so tentative, a hoarse edge to the words that showed his own fear —and somehow bolstered her confidence. If he was afraid...then was he feeling the same way?

She fought the urge to play it cool, to pretend. She'd spent so much time in her life pretending, and it had gotten her nowhere. She had to be honest and straight with this man. It was worth the risk. He was worth it.

"I'm thinking about how I didn't expect to be here," she said softly. "In a lot of different ways."

He pressed his lips together, but it took all of half a second for a grin to break out on his boyish face. "That sounds like a good thing."

She laughed, poking him in the ribs lightly. "Of course it's a good thing." Her fear began to melt away, that heaviness dissipating, confidence building, excitement bubbling up inside of her. "I had an amazing time. And I don't want this to be the only time."

His eyes shone. "Me either," he admitted, voice thick. "I...ugh, this is so corny, but...it feels like I'm a whole new person."

"No." She shook her head. "The person you've really been all along." She curled her hand around the back of his neck, running her fingers through his hair softly. "I get it, I feel the same way. Like I've been just, I don't know, coasting?"

He nodded, the movement rustling against the pillow. "I've spent so much of my life pretending to be something I'm not, attracting the type of people who didn't see me for who I am." He swallowed hard. "You saw me. You see me. I felt all through this that you knew exactly what I needed in every moment."

"You're very expressive," she teased.

He playfully booped her nose. "I don't think so. I think you can read me because we're compatible." His cheeks pinked, and he glanced away from her. "I feel safe with you."

Annika brought her hands to his face, prompting him to look at her, however hesitantly. "Don't be embarrassed to say that to me," she said firmly. "You *are* safe with me." She kissed him, brushing her lips against his so softly, but not quite chastely.

Ben took in a deep breath as if he were inhaling her essence, the power passing between them like a charge, filling his lungs with her courage.

"This is terrifying," he whispered breathlessly when they parted, "and not because of the dynamic...I just...I feel so connected to you in a way that I never have with anyone. I probably shouldn't say it, especially not on a first date but...I don't think I can *not* say it. It wouldn't be fair to you."

Tears sprang to her eyes, shock rippling through her at the sensation. Her first instinct upon hearing him whisper the words that she'd been carrying inside of her, trying to figure out how to verbalize, had been tears. Her chest clenched again, and she brushed her thumb across his strong jaw, taking in every slope and curve of his beautiful face.

"I don't know if it's just because it's my first time doing-- all this--but I just--" he rambled, and she put her thumb over his mouth.

"Sorry, I didn't mean to not respond," she said earnestly. "I got distracted by you and forgot how to make words. I get it, though, I feel the same way. Hit me like a gut punch a few times during, and then after...this is..." She let out a deep *whoosh* of breath and shook her head, laughing. "Something else."

He pressed his forehead to hers, eyes fluttering closed. "Thank you for not kicking me out for being so forward."

She couldn't help but laugh. "You, forward? I pretty much demanded you walk me home."

"I ruined your date night," he countered.

"I pushed the security button just to see you."

"I ducked out on work so I could sneak into an event to see *you*."

She laughed again. "So we're both forward."

"I think we both knew what we wanted," Ben said, curling some of her hair behind her ear.

Annika scooched in a bit closer, pressing her skin back up against his. "I think we both know what we want," she corrected. "Now be a good boy and fuck me again."

He grinned wickedly. "Yes, ma'am."

END

WANT MORE STEAM? Sign up for my mailing list at https://emilyshurricane.com/free-ebook for a free spicy ebook!

About the Author

Emily S Hurricane writing as Iris Trovao

Emily is an east-coast Canadian thirtysomething mom of two humans and a furbaby. Her lumbersexual husband doesn't actually work in lumber anymore, but he still wears the plaid and the beard.

As well as authoring, she's a freelance editor and ghostwriter. Her books range in genre from Romance and Erotica to Horror and Science Fiction, and everything in between.

When she's not writing and/or momming, she's sipping espresso, crocheting, and listening to audiobooks.

You can find Emily and her collected works at emilyshurricane.com. If you want access to her entire backlist and early content, check out her Patreon at patreon.com/emilyshurricane.

Other Stories

Romance
As Iris Trovao
Wrong Number
Shotgun Cowgirl
Shotgun Wedding
Shotgun Sheriff
On His Knees

Paranormal Fantasy
As Emily S Hurricane
The Beginning of the End
Southern Ice
A Tale of Two Fathers
The Sea Meets The Sky
Northern Fire
The Wolf and the Barista
King of Demons

Serial Stories
On Radish Fiction

OTHER STORIES

Bloodlines
Her Tyrant Alpha
Shotgun Cowgirl
King of Demons

Anthologies
Love at First Sip, A Romance Anthology (*Emily S Hurricane*)
Secrets, An Erotic Anthology (*Maria Rush*)
Don't Read This Book After Dark Vol. 1, A Horror Anthology (*Alice J. Taylor*)
Don't Read This Book After Dark Vol. 2, A Horror Anthology (*Alice J. Taylor*)

BDSM Erotica
As Valerie Gale
Bag of Tricks
With Friends Like These
Princess
Hard Lessons
Tasting Mrs. Carter
Internal Affairs
Quiet, Please!
Caught and Punished
Dined and Dominated
Training the Guitarist

Menage/RH/Poly Erotica
As Arlene Tempest
Behind the Curtain
A Blond, a Brunette, and a Redhead
The House Always Wins
Playing Doctor
Long Distance
Choke Hold

Sapphic Erotica
As Maria Rush
The Boss' Daughter
The Boxer and the Bartender
Cherry Pie
Rev Your Engines
Unwrapping Santa

Paranormal Erotica
As Ophelia Storm
Black, White, and Red All Over
The Witch and the Fairy
The Beast and the Convent
Undead and Dominated
Holycanthropy!
Wolfensaint
And Then There Were Nun

Erotica Bundles
A Bundle of Moresomes
Dominated by Him
Bad Habits
Dominated by Her
All Hers

Find all of these and more as well as early access to upcoming stories at
 patreon.com/emilyshurricane!

Printed in Great Britain
by Amazon